Dear Parent:

Congratulations! Your child is taking the first steps on an exciting journey. The destination? Independent reading!

STEP INTO READING® will help your child get there. The program offers books at five levels that accompany children from their first attempts at reading to reading success. Each step includes fun stories, fiction and nonfiction, and colorful art. There are also Step into Reading Sticker Books, Step into Reading Math Readers, and Step into Reading Phonics Readers—a complete literacy program with something to interest every child.

Learning to Read, Step by Step!

Ready to Read Preschool–Kindergarten
• big type and easy words • rhyme and rhythm • picture clues
For children who know the alphabet and are eager to begin reading.

Reading with Help Preschool–Grade 1
• basic vocabulary • short sentences • simple stories
For children who recognize familiar words and sound out new words with help.

Reading on Your Own Grades 1–3
• engaging characters • easy-to-follow plots • popular topics
For children who are ready to read on their own.

Reading Paragraphs Grades 2–3
• challenging vocabulary • short paragraphs • exciting stories
For newly independent readers who read simple sentences with confidence.

Ready for Chapters Grades 2–4
• chapters • longer paragraphs • full-color art
For children who want to take the plunge into chapter books but still like colorful pictures.

STEP INTO READING® is designed to give every child a successful reading experience. The grade levels are only guides. Children can progress through the steps at their own speed, developing confidence in their reading, no matter what their grade.

Remember, a lifetime love of reading starts with a single step!

STEP INTO READING®

Tiger Is a Scaredy Cat

by Joan Phillips

illustrated by Norman Gorbaty

Random House 🏠 New York

Text copyright © 1986 by Joan Phillips. Illustrations copyright © 1986 by Norman Gorbaty.
All rights reserved under International and Pan-American Copyright Conventions.
Published in the United States by Random House Children's Books, a division of Random House, Inc.,
New York, and simultaneously in Canada by Random House of Canada Limited, Toronto.

www.stepintoreading.com

Educators and librarians, for a variety of teaching tools, visit us at
www.randomhouse.com/teachers

Library of Congress Cataloging-in-Publication Data
Phillips, Joan.
Tiger is a scaredy cat / by Joan Phillips ; illustrated by Norman Gorbaty.
p.   cm. — (Step into reading. A step 2 book)
SUMMARY: Tiger, a scaredy cat who is even afraid of the mice in his house,
conquers his fear in order to help Baby Mouse.
ISBN 0-394-88056-0 (trade) — ISBN 0-394-98056-5 (lib. bdg.)
[1. Courage—Fiction.   2. Cats—Fiction.   3. Mice—Fiction.]
I. Gorbaty, Norman, ill.   II. Title.   III. Series: Step into reading. Step 2 book.
PZ7.P5376   Ti   2003   [E]—dc21   2002014644

Printed in the United States of America   47 46 45 44 43 42 41 40 39 38

STEP INTO READING, RANDOM HOUSE, and the Random House colophon are registered
trademarks of Random House, Inc.

Tiger is big.

Tiger is strong.

But Tiger is not brave.

He is scared of dogs.

He is scared
of trucks.

He is scared
of the vacuum cleaner.

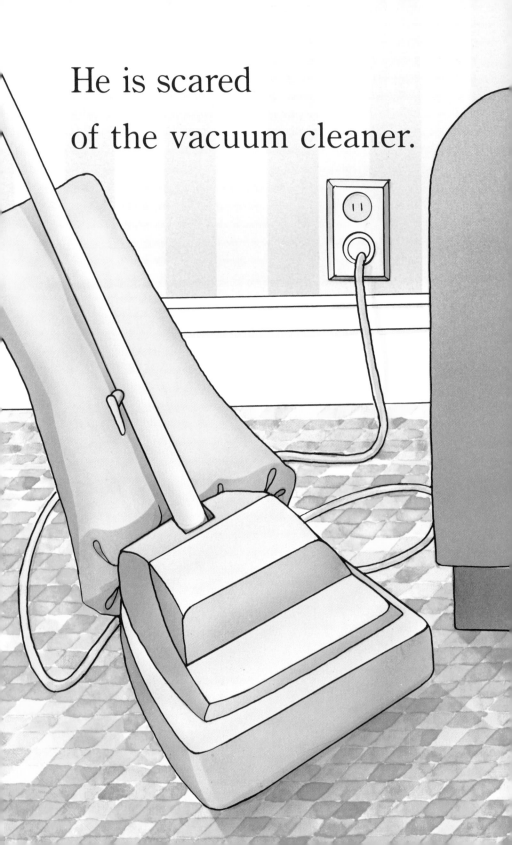

He is scared
of the dark.

Tiger is even scared
of the mice in his house.
What a scaredy cat!

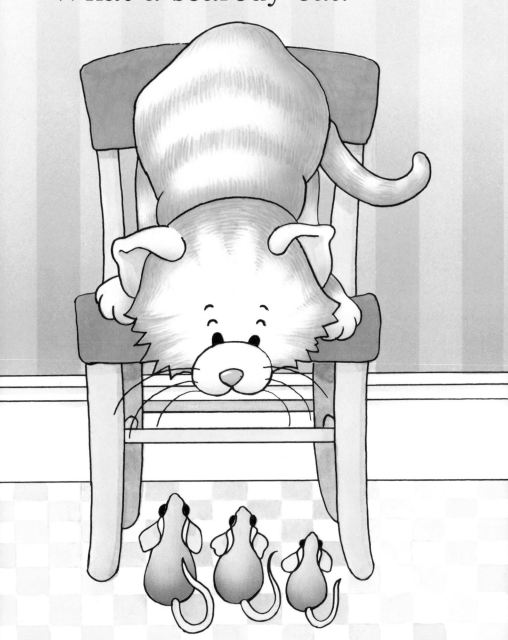

There is nothing scary here.

There are no dogs,

no trucks,

no vacuum cleaners,

no mice.

And it is very sunny.

Tiger takes a cat nap.

The mice take a walk.

They do not see the cat.

Now they see the cat.
The mice are scared.
They run away.

Tiger sees the mice.

He is scared.

He runs too.

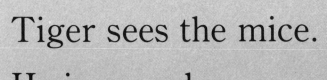

Baby Mouse falls.

"Waa! Waa!" he cries.

Tiger hears Baby Mouse.

"Waa! Waa!
I want to go home!"
cries Baby Mouse.
"Help me."

"No! I am too scared,"
says Tiger.

"Waa! Waa!
I want my mommy!"
cries Baby Mouse.
Tiger feels sorry
for Baby Mouse.

"Do not cry.
I will help you."

Tiger has to go
by a truck.

He has to go
by a dog.

He has to go
by the vacuum cleaner.

He has to go
down the dark stairs.

Tiger is scared.
But he helps anyway.
"Here is your mommy,"
he says.

"My baby!"
says Mother Mouse.
"Thank you! Thank you!"
says Father Mouse.

What a brave cat Tiger is!